Note to parents, carers and teachers

Read it yourself is a series of modern stories, favourite characters and traditional tales written in a simple way for children who are learning to read. The books can be read independently or as part of a guided reading session.

Each book is carefully structured to include many high-frequency words vital for first reading. The sentences on each page are supported closely by pictures to help with understanding, and to offer lively details to talk about.

The books are graded into four levels that progressively introduce wider vocabulary and longer stories as a reader's ability and confidence grows.

Ideas for use

- Begin by looking through the book and talking about the pictures. Has your child heard this story before?

- Help your child with any words he does not know, either by helping him to sound them out or supplying them yourself.

- Developing readers can be concentrating so hard on the words that they sometimes don't fully grasp the meaning of what they're reading. Answering the puzzle questions at the end of the book will help with understanding.

For more information and advice on Read it yourself and book banding, visit www.ladybird.com/readityourself

Book
Band
6

Level 2 is ideal for children who have received some reading instruction and can read short, simple sentences with help.

Special features:

Frequent repetition of main story words and phrases

Short, simple sentences

Careful match between story and pictures

Large, clear type

Lady Rob had a trick. "Help!" she said. "I cannot get in to my house!"

"Swooperman to the rescue!" said Swooperman. He swooped up to get in to the house.

10

11

Lady Rob ran out of the bank with all the money.

She laughed and said, "You will not swoop again, Swooperman!"

20

21

Educational Consultant: Geraldine Taylor
Book Banding Consultant: Kate Ruttle

LADYBIRD BOOKS

UK | USA | Canada | Ireland | Australia
India | New Zealand | South Africa

Ladybird Books is part of the Penguin Random House group of companies
whose addresses can be found at global.penguinrandomhouse.com.

ladybird.com

Penguin
Random House
UK

First published 2015
001

Printed in China

A CIP catalogue record for this book is available from the British Library

ISBN: 978–0–723–29526–6

Superhero Max

Written by Mandy Ross
Illustrated by Ed Myer

Max was a boy, but he was a superhero as well. He was Swooperman!

When Max was Swooperman, he had swoop boots to stop baddies and rescue people.

Ricky Rob was a baddie.
He robbed banks.

Lady Rob was Ricky's mum
and she was a baddie, too!

She robbed banks with Ricky.

Lady Rob had a trick. "Help!" she said. "I cannot get in to my house!"

"Swooperman to the rescue!" said Swooperman. He swooped up to get in to the house.

11

"Thank you, Swooperman!" said Lady Rob. "Have some tea."

Swooperman had some tea, but it was trick tea and it made him go to sleep.

Lady Rob got his swoop boots!

"I want the swoop boots,
Mum," said Ricky Rob.
"I want to rob the bank!"

"No!" said Lady Rob.
"I will rob the bank!"

"One, two, swoop!"
said Lady Rob, and
she swooped away.

A boy ran to Swooperman.
"You cannot sleep," he said.
"Lady Rob is going to rob
the bank!"

"Swooperman to the rescue!"
said Swooperman.

But he had no swoop boots.
He could not swoop!

Swooperman ran to the bank. When he got there he said, "Lady Rob! Stop!"

But Lady Rob was going to rob the bank.

Lady Rob ran out of the bank with all the money.

She laughed and said, "You will not swoop again, Swooperman!"

Lady Rob and Ricky Rob swooped away with all the money.

"You cannot stop us, Swooperman!" laughed the two baddies.

"But I can stop the swoop boots," said Swooperman.

Swooperman made the boots swoop down. The boots and the baddies swooped back down to a policeman.

25

"Got you, Lady Rob! Got you, too, Ricky Rob!" said Swooperman. "You will not rob banks again."

"Two baddies in one swoop!" said the policeman. "Thank you, Swooperman. You ARE a superhero!"

Max was back in his house.

"Help, Swooperman! Help!" said a boy.

Superhero Max got his swoop boots and said, "Swooperman to the rescue!"

How much do you remember about the story of Superhero Max? Answer these questions and find out!

- **What makes Swooperman go to sleep?**

- **Who takes Swooperman's swoop boots?**

- **Who robs the bank?**

- **How does Swooperman catch the baddies?**

Look at the pictures and match them
to the story words.

bank

Lady Rob

Ricky Rob

swoop boots

Swooperman

Tick the books you've read!

Level 2

Level 3